RANGER in TIME

Disaster on the Titanic

THE RANGER IN TIME SERIES

Disaster on the Titanic

KATE MESSNER

illustrated by
KELLEY McMORRIS

Scholastic Inc.

Text copyright © 2019 by Kate Messner
Illustrations by Kelley McMorris, copyright © 2019 Scholastic Inc.

This book is being published simultaneously in hardcover by Scholastic Press.

Library of Congress Cataloging-in-Publication Data
Names: Messner, Kate, author. | McMorris, Kelley, illustrator. | Messner, Kate. Ranger in time ; 9.
Title: Disaster on the Titanic / Kate Messner ; illustrated by Kelley McMorris.
Description: New York : Scholastic Inc., 2019. | Series: Ranger in time , 9 | Summary: This time the mysterious box transports the golden retriever Ranger back to the shipyards of Belfast in 1912, where a ship is being prepared for her maiden voyage, and when he saves young Patrick Murphy from being crushed by falling boards, Ranger expects to be transported home; when he is not, he knows that somehow his job is not finished — but then, Ranger has never heard of the Titanic, and knows nothing of the fate that awaits Patrick, and all the other people on board.
Identifiers: LCCN 2018013837
Subjects: LCSH: Titanic (Steamship) — Juvenile fiction. | Golden retriever — Juvenile fiction. | Time travel — Juvenile fiction. | Shipwrecks — North Atlantic Ocean — Juvenile fiction. | Adventure stories. | North Atlantic Ocean — Juvenile fiction. | CYAC: Titanic (Steamship) — Fiction. | Golden retriever — Fiction. | Dogs — Fiction. | Time travel — Fiction. | Shipwrecks — Fiction. | Survival — Fiction. | Adventure and adventurers — Fiction. | LCGFT: Action and adventure fiction.
Classification: LCC PZ10.3.M5635 Di 2019 | DDC 813.6 [Fic] — dc23
LC record available at https://lccn.loc.gov/2018013837

ISBN 978-1-338-13398-1

10 9 8 7 6 5 4 3 2 1   19 20 21 22 23

Printed in the United States of America   40
First printing 2019

Book design by Ellen Duda and Maeve Norton

*For Linda Aloi and the readers of
Cobbles Elementary School*

Chapter 1

LOOK OUT BELOW!

Patrick Murphy hurried through the dark streets of Belfast. If he arrived late for work at the Harland and Wolff shipyard, the gate would be closed. He'd lose his pay for the day.

Patrick picked up his pace. When he turned the corner and saw the open gate, his heart filled with relief. He'd made it!

Patrick stopped at the time office, picked up his board, and tucked it into his pocket. The worker number stamped on the small piece of wood ensured that he'd get credit for the hours he'd worked when he turned it in at the end of the day.

The yard hummed with activity as men streamed in from all over the city. The shadow of the big ship towered over them.

Patrick had grown up in this shipyard, right along with the *Titanic*. He remembered visiting his father at work when he was a little boy. He'd peek in the big windows of the Harland and Wolff drawing room to watch Mr. Andrews and the other designers making plans for the biggest boats in the world. Patrick longed to stand at the desks with them, imagining and drawing such amazing ships.

They started work on the *Titanic* in 1909, when Patrick was eleven. First came the gantry — a huge structure with cranes, elevators, and walkways. It was the scaffolding from which the men would build. Beneath the gantry, they'd laid the great ship's keel. Then came the framing.

On the morning of Patrick's twelfth birthday, his father had placed two new pennies in his hand before he left for work. "Hold on to them until I get home," he said. "We'll go out together to buy a sweet."

That was the day a section of staging collapsed in the shipyard. Patrick's father was killed in a fall. *He's away to the other yard*, the shipbuilders whispered.

Patrick tucked the pennies in a little cloth pouch. He hid them away in his trunk and promised himself he'd never spend them.

But Patrick and his mother needed money to eat, so they went to work in one of Belfast's linen mills.

It was dangerous and dusty. Patrick's mother developed a cough. Soon, it became so bad she couldn't work anymore.

Patrick needed a job that could support both of them. So when he turned thirteen, he went back to the shipyard, where crews continued to work on the *Titanic*. Patrick joined a riveting team that fastened great steel plates onto the ship's skeleton. But now that work was mostly finished, Patrick took on other jobs — painting and running supplies. Everyone was busy getting ready for the ship's launch, just two months away.

Sometimes, Mr. Andrews himself would tour the shipyard. The pockets of his blue jacket were always stuffed with plans. Patrick wished he could stop work for just a moment on those mornings. He'd love to unroll the drawings and talk with the shipbuilder about what he might imagine next.

But today, there was too much work for daydreaming. "Move along, Murphy!" the foreman called.

Patrick hurried to his work site. Today, they'd start building the slipway, the big ramp that would run up to the ship and under the keel. On launch day, the *Titanic* would slide down that ramp into the water, and everyone would cheer.

"Watch yourself!" someone called as a crane unloaded a pile of timbers beside the men. Patrick unhooked the bundle, and the crane's arm rose up to get more.

"Over here!" the foreman called. One by one, Patrick and the other men lifted the enormous timbers and walked them into place.

"More on the way!" someone called as the crane's arm swung their way again.

Patrick wiped his brow with his sleeve. His stomach growled. How long was it until the morning break? Breakfast was only bread and tea, but it would be better than working with an empty belly.

While Patrick waited for the next bundle of timbers, he let his eyes close, just for a moment, and listened. He loved the music of a ship coming to life — the banging and rattling of steel on steel.

But then another sound rang out from above. A deep, booming voice.

"Look out below!"

Chapter 2

ALL ABOARD!

"Did you find your life jackets yet?" Mom asked Luke and Sadie. They were getting ready to go for a boat ride with their friends the Tarars.

"Not yet," Luke said. "I'll look in the shed. Want to come outside with me, Ranger?"

Ranger barked and followed Luke to the door. Ranger always wanted to go outside.

While Luke ran to the shed to look for life jackets, Ranger wandered over to Mom's garden. There were always good smells there — birds and bugs, plants and dirt, and . . .

Squirrel!

Ranger looked around. There it was, over by the squash plants!

Ranger chased the squirrel through the garden. He chased it past the tomatoes and carrots. He chased it across the lawn, around the picnic table, and up a tree. The squirrel sat on a branch, chattering down at him.

"Nice try, Ranger," Luke said as he walked by with the life jackets. "Maybe you'll get one next time."

Ranger wasn't worried about that. He didn't really want to catch a squirrel anyway. He just loved chasing them. That was why he wasn't an official search-and-rescue dog.

Ranger had gone through lots of special training with Luke and Dad. He'd learned all about helping people who were missing or in trouble. He'd learned how to find people by following their scent. He'd practiced searching

on rainy days and windy days. He'd practiced searching in the woods and in buildings. Ranger was very good at finding people and helping.

But he was not so good at ignoring squirrels. To pass your search-and-rescue-dog test, you had to ignore everything except the command. You had to ignore hot dogs that people left on the lawn. You had to ignore good smells and birds and squirrels.

When Ranger was taking his test, a squirrel had raced across the grass right in front of him. Ranger chased it. He knew Luke was just hiding, pretending to be missing. He wouldn't have chased the squirrel if a person was really in trouble.

But that didn't matter. Ranger didn't pass his search-and-rescue-dog test, so now he chased squirrels instead.

This squirrel wasn't coming down, though, so Ranger went to find Luke. He was in the driveway with his friends Zeeshan and Noreen. The Tarar family had just arrived. Luke and Sadie and their parents were loading everything into the car to go to the marina.

"It's too bad you don't like boats, Ranger," Luke said, giving Ranger a pat on the head. "But we won't be gone long." He let Ranger back inside the house, and then the families drove away.

Ranger padded around for a while to see if anyone had dropped food before they left. He licked up some cookie crumbs from the kitchen floor. Then he curled up in a patch of sunshine to nap.

When Ranger woke, the sunny patch had moved. He went to the mudroom for a drink of water and heard a quiet humming coming from his dog bed. He walked over and pawed at his blanket until he uncovered the first aid kit he'd dug up in Mom's garden on another day. The humming was coming from the old metal box. It was louder now.

Ranger knew that sound. He'd heard it before, always when someone needed his help. One time, the old first aid kit had transported him to an explorers' ship on a frozen sea. Another time, it had taken him to help a girl in a trembling, fiery city. It had sent him on long, dangerous journeys, to a flooded neighborhood, and to a battlefield on a faraway beach.

All around the first aid kit in Ranger's dog bed were his treasures, gifts from the children he met on those journeys. There was an old quilt square from a boy named Sam, a feather from a girl named Sarah, and a purple bandanna from Clare, the girl in the flood.

Now the first aid kit was humming again.

Ranger nuzzled the worn leather strap over his head, and the humming got louder. The box grew warm at his throat. Light spilled from the cracks. It grew brighter and brighter, until Ranger had to close his eyes. He felt as if he were being squeezed through a hole in the sky.

And then the box was quiet.

Ranger opened his eyes. New sounds pounded in his ears. Clanging and banging. Crashing and rattling. Deep voices shouting.

The air smelled of sawdust and steel, paint and sweat and the sea.

Above him, a huge machine creaked and swung its metal arm. A messy heap of wooden boards dangled overhead. They looked as if they might wiggle loose any second. Men rushed everywhere, carrying paint buckets, tools, and lumber.

In the middle of it all, a boy a little older than Luke stood with his eyes closed.

Then there was a terrible cracking sound from above. And a voice bellowed, "Look out below!"

Chapter 3

BIG NEWS

Ranger leaped at the boy and knocked him off balance. The boy tumbled backward, trying to catch his footing. He fell onto his backside in the sawdust as the timbers from above crashed to the ground.

"Everyone all right?" someone shouted.

A big man reached out and pulled Patrick to his feet. "You're lucky that dog knocked you on your rear end. Those timbers would have cracked your head open."

Patrick looked at the splintered wooden planks. Then he looked at Ranger. "I don't know where you came from, dog. But thank you." He gave Ranger a scratch behind his ear.

"Back to work!" the foreman shouted.

Ranger stayed out of the way while the men hammered, painted, and checked the ship's engines and boilers. All day long, he watched over Patrick.

When the dinner horn sounded at the end of the day, Ranger followed Patrick to the time office to return the little wooden board that would give him credit for the hours he'd worked.

Patrick almost tripped over Ranger when he turned to leave. "Whose dog are you?" All around them, workmen streamed down the gangway, heading home. No one seemed to be looking for a dog.

"Well then," Patrick said, "you'll just have to come home with me."

So that's what Ranger did. That night, he

slept by the stove in the tiny apartment with Patrick and his mother. The next morning, he followed Patrick to the shipyard and watched over him again. He did the same thing the next day . . . and the next . . . and the next. There wasn't much to eat, but the men at the shipyard gave Ranger little scraps from their lunches.

Ranger stayed with Patrick while the men finished the slipway and painted the sides of the ship. He kept watch while they prepared mooring ropes, ladders, and fenders. He worried when Patrick's work involved heavy machines or unstable beams. There was danger in the air every day but nothing Ranger could really do to help. Every night, he curled up by the stove with his first aid kit tucked in quietly beside him. He wondered when he'd finish his work here, and when he'd get to go home.

The final days before the *Titanic*'s launch were the busiest of all. There was so much to be done before the ship would slide into the water for the first time! After that, it would be towed to the wharf, where workers would spend months outfitting the great ship for its maiden voyage.

Patrick and Ranger arrived at the shipyard before the sun rose each morning. The men spread grease on the slipway they'd built. They took soundings in the channel to make sure the *Titanic* wouldn't run aground.

On the morning of May 31, 1911, a rocket exploded over the harbor, warning small boats to get out of the way. It was time for the *Titanic* to launch!

Black smoke poured from the ship's funnels. A White Star Line flag flew over the bow. Men pulled off their caps, and ladies waved their handkerchiefs as the ship slid into the water.

"Look at that," Patrick whispered, stroking Ranger's fur as they watched.

"And we built her right here in Belfast," another man said.

Patrick's heart swelled with pride. It was the greatest ship to ever set sail across the Atlantic. The fastest, too. And he had helped build it.

The Belfast launch was a day of celebration. Pride in a job well done. But when Ranger went home with Patrick that night, the first aid kit still sat quietly by the stove. That meant he had more work to do.

So did Patrick. He set to work at the wharf, preparing the *Titanic* for its maiden voyage. There, workers installed the ship's boilers and funnels. They painted and moved furniture and hauled supplies. Ranger lost track of the days until, one night, Patrick hurried home to tell his mother the most exciting news of all.

"I'm going on the *Titanic*'s maiden voyage!" Patrick said. He felt as if his heart might burst out of his chest and leave tonight.

"My heavens! How is that possible?" his mother asked.

"They've chosen some men from the shipyard," Patrick said, "in case anything needs to be fixed along the way. And I'll be helping out as a steward, tending to the passengers."

His mother's brow wrinkled. "But it's a long trip. So far . . ."

"On such a fast ship, I'll be home before you know it," Patrick promised. "And I may get promoted when I return to the shipyard. Wouldn't it be nice to have more than bread and tea for supper?"

His mother's eyes shined with tears. "Your father would be so proud," she said. "He'd have loved to see that ship sail. I'll pray for your safety."

Late that night, after his mother went to bed, Patrick pulled a cloth pouch from his trunk. He turned it upside down and shook the two pennies from his father into his palm. They still looked brand-new. And they'd turned out to be lucky after all.

Patrick stared out the window with Ranger at his side. "Can you believe it, dog?" he whispered, stroking Ranger's fur. "We're going to New York!"

Ranger leaned into Patrick's rough hand. He understood something big was about to happen. And wherever Patrick was going, he needed to go, too.

Chapter 4

BOUND FOR NEW YORK!

On the morning of April 2, 1912, the *Titanic* set sail for the English city of Southampton. Patrick stood beside Ranger on the deck as Belfast grew smaller in the distance.

"We're off to New York, dog!" Patrick said, scratching Ranger behind his ear. "We will be soon, at least. First, we'll go to England and France to pick up passengers. Then back to Ireland for one last stop in Queenstown. A little over a week from now, we'll be setting off across the Atlantic!"

"Murphy!" called one of the crewmen. "Let's go! There's painting yet to do."

Ranger followed Patrick down some stairs and through a long hallway to a propped-open door. Inside was a fancy bed, desk, and chairs. It smelled of polished wood and fresh paint. "You'd better wait here," Patrick told Ranger. "They won't want dogs in the first-class cabins."

Ranger sat in the hallway. The big ship was full of interesting smells. Salt water and steel and the sweat of all the men still working. Also . . . cat?

Ranger sniffed the air.

Definitely cat.

He followed the cat smell down the hallway to a storage closet where a mother cat and her new kittens were curled up next to a crate of potatoes.

Ranger barked.

The cat hissed at him.

Patrick appeared in the doorway. "I see you've met Jenny!" he said, and reached down to stroke the cat's fur. She purred and leaned into Patrick's hand. "She's our ship's cat." Patrick stood up and patted Ranger's head, too. "Don't worry," he whispered. "The kittens may be cute, but you're still my favorite."

Two days later, the *Titanic* arrived in Southampton to a flurry of activity. Ranger kept an eye on Patrick, but mostly he tried to stay out of the way while workers loaded supplies. Then came the passengers — a stream of men and women in dark, fancy clothes.

Some of them brought dogs! They were mostly fluffy little things. But one tall man with a mustache boarded with an Airedale he called Kitty. Ranger also saw a wrinkly dog with a scrunched-up face.

"I picked him up in Paris," the dog's owner told another man. "French bulldogs are popular there."

Patrick carried luggage for wealthy first-class passengers who had purchased expensive tickets with fancy rooms and fine dining. He directed third-class people where to go, too. Their tickets cost much less, so their cabins were simpler, more crowded, and on the lower decks.

The night before they left Southampton, Ranger saw the Jenny cat again. She was carrying her kittens off the ship, one by one. It looked like only the dogs would be going to New York. That was fine with Ranger. He didn't like being hissed at anyway.

When the *Titanic* left England, crowds stood in the sunshine, waving handkerchiefs to say good-bye. It was four hours to Cherbourg, France, where the ship dropped anchor a mile offshore. Cherbourg's pier wasn't big enough for the *Titanic*, so another boat called the *Nomadic* had to ferry new passengers out to board the big ship.

Many of these new passengers spoke different languages. Some had come from villages in Lebanon, another crew member told Patrick. They were going to start new lives in America.

At the edge of the crowd, Ranger saw two children who looked a little older than Luke and Sadie. The girl held a small rag doll with black hair like hers. They seemed as if they might be lost.

Ranger trotted over and nuzzled the boy's hand. The boy jumped back, but his younger sister knelt and stroked Ranger's fur.

Soon, Patrick hurried over. "Where's your family?" he asked the children.

"They are in America," the boy said in a small voice. "They left us behind until they could find jobs and a place to live."

"Oh! Are you from one of the villages in Lebanon?" Patrick asked.

The girl nodded. "Our uncle taught us English," she said. "To be ready for America. Teta learned, too."

"Teta?" Patrick looked around.

"Our grandmother," the girl said. "But she is sick right now, so we are going to America on our own. She will come later." The girl seemed fine with that, but her brother's face was full of worry.

Patrick understood what it was like to feel alone. "Don't worry," he said. "We'll take good care of you on the *Titanic*. What are your names?"

"Maryam," the girl said. "I'm nine and my brother, Hamad, is ten."

"I'm Patrick, and I'm part of the crew. I also helped build this ship." Patrick couldn't help standing a little taller when he said that.

"Can you show us where our cabin is?" Hamad said, holding out their tickets.

"Sure, but it'll have to be in a little while, when things quiet down," Patrick said. "You're on E deck, and I'm assigned to work up here while people board."

The children waited with Patrick as the other passengers boarded. When everyone was finally settled, Patrick said, "Let's find your cabin now, all right?"

Patrick and Ranger led the children down to the *Titanic*'s E deck, two floors above the ship's engine and boiler rooms. Hamad and Maryam were in a cabin with a family of six people from their village. The man and woman welcomed them.

This crowded room looked nothing like the first-class cabins. It was smaller and simpler, and filled with noise and activity. The mother was unpacking things she'd brought from home. One of the older brothers began playing a hand drum he held under his arm.

"A durbakkah!" Maryam said, and ran over to play with him.

"Have a good voyage," Patrick said.

"You too!" Maryam called. Hamad waved from his bunk.

Patrick walked down a long hall to the cabin he shared with other crew members.

"Just one more stop before we set off across the Atlantic, dog!" Patrick said, yawning. He climbed into his bunk and went to sleep with Ranger curled up at his feet.

The next day, when the ship docked in Queenstown, peddlers came on board to sell

Irish lace and other last-minute goods. Then finally, the *Titanic* left Ireland with hundreds of seagulls flying in its wake.

"We're off to New York!" Patrick told Ranger.

Ranger sniffed the salty air and leaned in to let Patrick pet him. He'd been away from Luke and Sadie for so long. Maybe now his work was almost done. How far was it to New York? Ranger didn't know. But he hoped that when they arrived, he'd finally get to go home.

Chapter 5

DANGER ON DECK!

For the next two days, Ranger followed Patrick around the ship as it surged through the waves. The men from the shipyard who had come along on the maiden voyage helped with whatever needed to be done — assisting first-class passengers, peeling potatoes, delivering messages.

Whenever he had a moment, Patrick went down to the third-class cabins to visit his new friends, Hamad and Maryam. The people from their village welcomed him and Ranger with figs from their trees back home. Most didn't speak English, but those who did told Patrick how they'd traveled on donkeys to Beirut, sailed from there to Marseille, and then taken a train to Cherbourg to board the big ship. Patrick told them how he had helped build the *Titanic* back in Belfast, piece by piece, from her propeller to the funnels that towered over the deck.

"But would you like to know a secret?" Patrick said. "Only three of the four funnels are connected to the boilers. The fourth is just for show, to make the ship look more powerful."

"Isn't the ship powerful enough?" Hamad asked.

"She certainly is," Patrick said. "There's talk that we could set a new speed record to New York!"

At the end of each night, Patrick went back to the crew's sleeping quarters. He kept the pouch with his father's two shiny pennies under his pillow. How proud his father would be if he could see Patrick now. *That's my boy,* he'd say. *Sailing clear across the wide ocean so you can care for your mother when you get home.*

Ranger curled up at the foot of Patrick's bunk at night and let the hum of the ship lull him to sleep. Even though Ranger didn't usually like boats, this big one was different — strong and steady and not at all tippy. Still, Ranger dreamed of his dog bed in the mudroom. He dreamed of squirrels and bacon and Luke and Sadie. And when he'd get to go home.

On Sunday, April 14, Patrick was called to help serve dinner in the first-class dining room. There were oysters and poached salmon, duckling and lamb and beef. Dessert was a spread of pudding, ice cream, and éclairs.

Ranger wasn't allowed in the dining room, so he climbed the stairs to the top of the ship and wandered the boat deck while Patrick was busy with dinner. One of the little yappy dogs always barked at Ranger, but most of the passengers were happy to see him. The ladies strolling on deck would pause and bend down to pat his head.

"Maryam!" someone shouted, just as Ranger was getting his neck scratched by a lady in a fluffy black hat.

Ranger turned and saw Hamad hurrying along the deck with a little rag doll.

"Maryam!" Hamad called, looking around. When he saw Ranger, he ran to him and dropped to his knees. "I can't find my sister!" he said.

Find? Ranger's ears perked up. He sniffed the little doll in Hamad's hands. It smelled of the third-class cabins — like smoke and spices. But there was another smell, too. The Maryam girl.

"She's wandered off. Can you help me find her?" the boy asked.

Find! Ranger knew that command from his search-and-rescue training. He'd always been able to find Luke in their practice sessions. He'd found him hiding in the woods on hot summer days and buried in the snow on winter mornings. He'd practiced finding Luke in wide-open meadows and on busy city blocks. But he'd never found anyone on a ship before.

Ranger sniffed the air. There were lots of people smells here. First-class men and women were rushing back to their cabins. They smelled of soap and perfume and the greasy meat they'd eaten for supper. Another smell hung over the boat deck, too. Ranger tipped his nose to the dark sky and sniffed the brisk, icy air. It smelled cold and fishy and sharp. But there was no Maryam smell.

Ranger led Hamad to the back of the boat and looked down to the deck below, where third-class passengers could walk in the open air at the boat's stern.

It was late, and the sky was dark. The night air was too cold for stargazing. All the passengers had gone to their cabins. The deck was empty.

"She's not here. I'm going to find help," Hamad said as he turned and walked away.

Just as Ranger was about to follow him, he caught a scent on the wind. But then it was gone.

Ranger walked all along the railing. He kept sniffing the cold air, searching for the Maryam smell.

Finally . . . *there!*

Ranger looked down at the empty deck.

There were no people — only a big crane that the crew used to move baggage sometimes. Earlier, some of the boys from third class had been climbing it, shimmying out on its long arm and then dropping down to the deck. They'd raced around, playing and climbing until their fathers made them stop.

But the boys were gone now. And Maryam was nowhere to be found. Every time Ranger caught her scent, it disappeared again. The smell was too scattered for him to follow. Where was she?

Ranger sniffed the air and barked. Then he heard a high, scared voice.

"Help! Please! I'm up here!"

Chapter 6

CLIMBING HIGH

Ranger looked down. Maryam had climbed out almost to the tip of the crane's arm. She was hugging the metal and looked like she'd been there awhile. Her hands were chapped and raw in the cold ocean air. Her face was streaked with tears.

"I'm stuck!" Maryam shouted. She clung to the crane with one arm and tugged at her skirt with the other. The fabric was caught in the machinery.

Ranger barked. He couldn't help Maryam. He didn't know how to get down to the deck below. There were no stairs. Even if he jumped, he couldn't climb the big machine and get her down. But he could bring someone who would.

Ranger took off running across the deck. He bounded down three flights of stairs, to the saloon deck, where Patrick had been working.

The first-class passengers had all gone to bed, but a few stewards remained, cleaning up dessert dishes and straightening chairs.

There! Ranger saw Patrick collecting teacups on a big tray. He ran up and barked.

Patrick jumped and almost dropped the tray. The cups and saucers rattled and clinked together. "What are you doing, dog?" Patrick's voice sounded cross. He put the tray down and reached for Ranger's collar. Ranger darted away from him.

Patrick followed him. Ranger barked and took a few steps down the hallway. He ran back to Patrick and jumped up on him. Then he ran down the hallway again.

"What is it, dog?" Patrick asked. "What's wrong?" He followed Ranger through the reception area and up the grand staircase.

Ranger led Patrick to the back of the ship. This time, he caught Maryam's scent in a hallway and followed it up to the deck where he'd seen her earlier. As soon as they stepped out into the cold night air, Ranger heard her crying. He barked and pawed at Patrick's leg.

Patrick looked way up at the arm of the crane. "Maryam!" he shouted. He took off his jacket and threw it on the deck. Then he hoisted himself onto the base of the crane and began to climb out its long arm.

Patrick's heart pounded. He'd been terrified of heights ever since his father's fall at the shipyard. He'd always found reasons to work

on the lower riveting and painting sites instead. But this was different.

"Hold on, Maryam! I'm coming!" Patrick called. He clung to the cold metal with his knees and reached for the next support. His hands were already numb from the cold, but he kept climbing.

The crane's arm wobbled every time Patrick moved. He forced himself not to look down. He kept his eyes on Maryam until, finally, he reached her and grabbed her icy hand.

"My dress!" she cried, looking down. Her skirt was caught between two pieces of metal, as if the big machine had taken a bite of it to hold her there.

"Hold on tight again. Just for a moment." Patrick let go of Maryam's hand. He wrapped his legs and one arm around the metal support and reached down as far as he could stretch. Finally, he felt the rough fabric in his hand. He gathered a handful and tugged. But the crane held on.

Patrick took a deep breath. He held the fabric tight and yanked as hard as he could. Finally, the skirt pulled free.

"There!" Patrick said. "Now let's climb down together." He shimmied backward down the crane's arm, stopping every few inches to guide Maryam's boot to the next foothold. When he made it to the base of the crane, he jumped down and reached up with both arms. Maryam leaned into them. He lifted her down onto the deck just as Hamad raced up the stairs with a man from their village.

"There you are!" Hamad said. He looked as if he couldn't decide whether to hug his sister or throw her overboard. "What were you doing?"

Maryam started to cry again. "I wanted to climb up like the boys did," she said. "I wanted to see onto the other deck." Ranger nuzzled

Maryam's hand until she knelt to pet him. That quieted her down.

Patrick and Ranger walked Hamad and Maryam back to the third-class cabins. It was nearly 11:30, and most of the families had gone to sleep. The music had stopped, and the instruments were all put away.

"Thank you," Hamad told Patrick.

"Thank him." Patrick nodded down at Ranger and gave him a scratch behind his ear. "He's the one who came to get me."

Hamad knelt and gave Ranger a tight hug. Then he stood and said good night to Patrick.

"Sleep well." As Patrick and Ranger turned to leave, the floor shuddered under their feet. A terrible scraping, crunching noise rattled the air. A grinding, grating sound, like a boat running up on rocks at the beach. Then doors opening and closing. And rushing, thumping footsteps.

"What is happening?" Hamad asked Patrick. "Did we bump something?"

"I'm not sure," Patrick said, but he had a terrible feeling. He opened the door and looked up and down the hallway. There didn't seem to be any warnings. "I'll go see, but I'm sure it's nothing. Try to get some sleep."

There were more footsteps rushing down the hallway above them. Then it was quiet again.

Too quiet. The engines had stopped.

Chapter 7

RISING WATERS

Patrick and Ranger hurried up to the deck. Everyone was talking at once.

"Is everything all right?"

"Why have we stopped?"

"Don't suppose it's anything much. Perhaps something to do with the machinery?"

"It's fine," one of the crewmen told a group of passengers. "You can go back to bed."

Some people returned to their cabins. Others huddled in their nightgowns on the deck.

"It was an iceberg, I tell you," someone said. "Saw the huge white mass myself when I looked out my porthole. Like a mountain on the sea."

"Come on, dog," Patrick said, hurrying toward the bow of the ship. "Let's see what we can learn."

Ranger followed Patrick, but the fur on his neck prickled. The air smelled icy and fishy and dangerous. Then Ranger felt something cold under his paw. He barked and stepped back.

Patrick bent down, picked up a chunk of ice, and sucked in his breath. "We must have hit ice," he whispered. He looked out into the darkness and tried to stay calm. *This ship was designed to sail through icy waters*, he reminded himself.

Sure enough, the engines chugged to life, and the ship started moving.

Patrick let out a whoosh of breath. "See, dog?" he said. "Everything is fine." Patrick had seen the *Titanic*'s plans himself, back at the shipyard. He'd counted the watertight compartments that would keep the great ship from sinking, no matter what. These were separate rooms on the lower levels of the ship, with special doors that could close in an emergency. That way, if water got into the ship's hull, it would be kept to one small area. It could never flood the entire ship.

So even though the *Titanic* had hit an iceberg, they would be fine. This might slow them down a bit, that was all.

Then the engines stopped again.

Two firemen came rushing up the steps. "She's flooding!" one of them shouted. "The watertight doors are closed, but who knows if it'll be enough. We had to dive under the door between boiler rooms five and six as it was closing. Made it just in time!"

"Go wake the first-class passengers," an officer told Patrick. "Get them up to the boat deck in their life jackets. Tell them it's just a precaution. We don't want to alarm them."

Patrick hesitated. "Is there cause for alarm?"

The officer pointed down the stairs. "Follow the order you've been given."

Patrick and Ranger hurried downstairs. They rushed up and down the first-class hallways. Ranger barked. Patrick pounded on cabin doors to wake people up. He helped them into their life jackets and sent them up to the deck.

Some people argued. "It's so dreadfully frigid out," one woman said.

"Is the ship actually taking on water?" one man asked Patrick. "Have you seen it for yourself?" He looked around his warm, dry cabin.

"No, sir," Patrick said. "But I've been told that everyone must head up to the boat deck now."

The man sighed. He pulled a coat on over his nightclothes and followed Patrick and Ranger down the hall and up the stairs.

The boat deck was getting crowded, but no one seemed very worried. Their only complaint was the temperature of the air. Was it really necessary to be out in this awful cold?

When Patrick finished waking the first-class passengers, he ran downstairs to see the damage for himself. It would be on the lower levels of the ship, near the mail room and one of the boiler rooms. Near Hamad and Maryam's cabin.

Ranger followed Patrick. With every flight of stairs they descended, the air smelled more dangerous. Like wet metal and seawater and ice.

When Patrick turned a corner to go down to the mail room, he stopped in his tracks.

Seawater had already climbed halfway up the staircase. The baggage area, mail room, and boiler rooms were all flooded.

Ranger saw the water, too, but he started down the stairs.

"No!" Patrick called. "Here, dog. We can't go down there. We have to go up to the deck."

But mixed in with the smell of seawater, soggy paper, and wet coal, Ranger had caught another scent. A person smell. He continued down the stairs until the water lifted him off his paws and he was paddling through the mail room.

"Dog! No!" Patrick shouted. He took another step down. Frigid water soaked his boots. "Come back!" he called to Ranger.

Ranger barked and kept paddling. The person smell was getting stronger.

There!

A young steward clung to a pipe in the corner of the room. Ranger barked at him.

"Get help, dog!" the young man shouted. He hadn't seen Patrick.

But it was Patrick who answered. "I'm here! It's all right. Let go and come to the stairs."

"I can't swim!" the man shouted.

"It's not that deep!" Patrick called. "Come on!"

But the man shook his head. His knuckles were white from gripping the pipe so tightly.

"Hold on, then. I'm coming!" Patrick took a deep breath and braced himself for the shock. Then he plunged into the icy flood.

Chapter 8

READY THE LIFEBOATS

The frigid water stole Patrick's breath away. It swallowed him up, all the way to his neck, and lapped at his chin. Patrick kept his head up. He pushed through the water, half swimming and half running to the corner of the mail room. He took hold of the young steward's arm. "Let go of the pipe now!" Patrick said. "The water's not over your head. I'll make sure you don't fall."

The man's eyes were wide with fear. His hands stayed clenched around the pipe. Ranger swam to him and used his nose to give the man's cheek a wet nudge. Finally, the man took a deep breath. He let go of the pipe and let Patrick guide him to the steps.

Ranger walked behind them, nudging the young man every time he looked back at the flood. They needed to get upstairs, away from this dangerous, rising water!

When they'd climbed up to the E deck, Patrick heard voices in the hallway. One of them sounded like Mr. Andrews from the shipyard. Patrick stopped and put a finger to his lips. The other young man nodded silently. They waited in the stairway as two men walked by.

"Well, three have gone already, Captain," one of the men said. "If six of the watertight compartments flood, she can't stay afloat."

The men's footsteps paused.

"Are you certain?" the other man asked.

"The weight of the seawater will sink the

bow, and the rest of the ship will follow," the first man said.

"How long do we have?"

"Perhaps two hours."

Patrick's stomach turned to stone. Two hours? Two hours before the greatest ship in the world would sink?

He turned to the young steward, who stood shivering in his wet clothes. His mouth hung open. He stared at Patrick. "Two hours, mate," the man whispered.

Patrick nodded. He swallowed hard. "Let's get to work."

They hurried up to the boat deck, where the *Titanic*'s lifeboats were tied. More passengers had come up from their cabins. Some dragged soggy suitcases behind them. Soon, the musicians arrived with their instruments. The band tuned up and began playing "Alexander's Ragtime Band." Passengers stood

in groups, listening, talking quietly, and laughing.

"All hands up!" someone shouted. "Get the lifeboats ready!"

The crewmen on deck sprung into action, but the passengers barely looked up from their conversations. Patrick couldn't stop staring. Had anyone told them the ship was going to sink? He wondered if the crew was working too hard to keep people calm. Would they even be willing to get in the lifeboats?

"Come on, mate!" Another crewman clapped Patrick on the shoulder. "Help ready the boats!"

Patrick and Ranger followed the man to the starboard side of the ship. Patrick began pulling the covers from the lifeboats.

"Release the grips on that one!" another man called. Patrick could barely hear him over the sound of steam pouring from the ship's funnels. "Release the grips!" the man shouted. Patrick did that and then began preparing ropes so the boat could be lowered. Other crew members prepared the davits, the cranes that would lower full lifeboats into the sea.

"The captain has given the order to swing out the boats!" someone called. "Bring up the passengers with life preservers on. Women and children first!"

Patrick looked at the crowd on the deck. There were twenty lifeboats in all. Could it possibly be enough for two thousand passengers and crew members?

There was no time to do the math. Patrick turned a crank to position lifeboat number seven alongside the ship. It swung on its ropes, and his heart crept up into his throat. He couldn't imagine climbing into such a little boat as it tipped back and forth, seventy feet above the ocean.

Patrick pushed the thought away. With so many passengers waiting, it would be a long time before it was his turn to board a lifeboat anyway. He held the boat steady as two of the passengers — a woman and her mother — climbed aboard.

One by one, Patrick helped twenty-eight people board lifeboat seven before it launched. There'd been room for more, but other passengers were staying back. They still didn't believe the ship might sink.

Patrick understood. It seemed impossible. But he remembered hearing Mr. Andrews in the E-deck hallway. "Maybe two hours . . ."

How long ago had that been? And how much time was left?

Chapter 9

NOT WITHOUT MY BROTHER!

"Lower away!" an officer shouted toward lifeboat five.

If Mr. Andrews was right, there was far too much work to be done in the minutes they had left before the ship sank. The crew was doing all they could to prepare lifeboats and load passengers. Mr. Andrews himself hurried around the deck, urging people to get into the boats.

They tried to board women and children first, but every time the crew turned away, men leaped into the boats. Women wailed for their husbands left behind on deck. Some threatened to get out of the boats if the men weren't allowed to join them. Eventually, the officer in charge let some men board lifeboat five as well.

Every time Patrick finished a job, there was another to be done. He was removing the sail and mast from a lifeboat to make room for more passengers when a scream came from lifeboat five, halfway down the side of the ship.

The crew had lowered one side faster than the other. The tilted boat threatened to dump all of its passengers into the freezing ocean. Patrick dropped the mast on the deck and rushed to help. Quickly, he and the other crewmen raised lifeboat five back to the boat deck until it was level again. More men scrambled aboard.

Patrick's heart thudded. He tried to catch his breath. He hadn't eaten supper, and his

knees threatened to give out under him. He reached out for the railing to steady himself, but sank to his knees. Ranger came up to nuzzle his shoulder.

Patrick sat down and stroked Ranger's fur, but it didn't calm his racing heart. His empty stomach twisted. The ship felt as if it might be tilting forward. Were they already starting to go down?

Ranger sniffed the night air. It still smelled of seawater and ice, but there were new smells, too. So many people, sweating under their thick coats. Danger and fear. And . . . bread?

Ranger left Patrick and sniffed along the railing. Yes . . . bread.

"What'd you find there, dog?" Patrick followed Ranger and picked up a sack from the deck. It was stuffed with loaves of bread. He looked around. There was more bread scattered near the lifeboats. The crew must have meant to load it on board. Patrick pulled a loaf from the sack. He tore off a hunk of bread and took a huge bite. He ripped off a second piece and gave it to Ranger. Then he leaned against the railing and stared up at the night sky.

A streak of light like a shooting star shot up from the ship. A shower of white sparks exploded over the *Titanic*. It lit up the faces of the passengers waiting on the deck. Patrick watched as their expressions changed from surprise to awe . . . to fear. Somehow, the emergency rocket launch had made them understand what they wouldn't listen to before. They were in danger. It was time to leave the ship.

Patrick scrambled to his feet and hurried to prepare the next lifeboat. Ranger couldn't help Patrick with his work, so he wandered among the passengers. Even in the chaos and fear, people reached down to stroke his damp fur or scratch his neck. Ranger stayed longest with the people whose hands were trembling the most.

He was getting a good ear scratch from a man in a top hat when a cry went up from the deck below. Ranger trotted to the rail to see what was happening. A mob of passengers crowded behind a gate that led up to the boat deck. They were arguing and surging forward. On the other side, a steward was pushing them back.

An officer shot a gun into the air. "Women and children only!" he shouted.

The steward reached over the gate to lift a little girl, but she pushed him away.

"No! I won't go!" she said. Ranger's ears perked up.

It was Maryam!

The steward said something. He caught the girl's hand and yanked her forward. Then he grabbed her under her arms and dragged her over the gate.

"No!" She pounded his shoulders and kicked at him. "Not without my brother!"

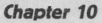

Chapter 10

LAST CHANCE TO LEAVE

Ranger ran to find Patrick. He weaved through a crowd of third-class passengers who had made their way up to the boat deck. He squeezed between first-class men and women in their coats and hats. Another rocket exploded over the ship.

Finally, Ranger found Patrick helping a young woman into her life jacket. He ran to him, barking, but Patrick didn't hear.

Ranger barked louder. Suddenly, the noise from the ship's great funnels quieted.

Passengers stared up at them, startled by the silence.

Ranger barked again. This time, Patrick looked over. Ranger pawed at his leg. Then he ran toward the gate where the children were.

"Hold on, dog!" Patrick was turning a crank, helping to lower another lifeboat.

As Patrick worked, he scanned the crowd. He hadn't seen Maryam or Hamad or anyone from their village yet. But maybe they were on the starboard side of the ship. Perhaps they'd already been lowered to safety. They were children, after all. Someone would be looking out for them now.

As soon as lifeboat three splashed into the water, Ranger was at Patrick's side, jumping up on him with both legs, running back and forth. Finally, Patrick followed Ranger through the crowd to the gate.

"I said no!" Maryam was still struggling with the frustrated crewman who was trying to move her toward the lifeboats. When she spotted Patrick, she shouted, "Tell him to let me go!"

Patrick hurried over. "What's this about?"

"I've been ordered to get the third-class women and children into boats," the steward said, still clutching Maryam's arm.

"But he won't let Hamad come!" Maryam's eyes shined with angry tears.

Patrick looked at the steward. "He's a boy."

"Almost a man," the steward said.

"I'm ten years old!" Hamad shouted.

The steward turned to Patrick and shook his head. "He looks older. They won't let him in the boats. If I send him up, he's likely to get shot."

Patrick swallowed hard. He'd seen crew

members firing pistols in the air, threatening men who tried to force their way onto boats. Would they shoot a child?

Before Patrick could argue any more, there was shouting on the deck. Four men were trying to force their way to the lifeboats.

The steward turned toward the commotion. As soon as he looked away, Hamad scrambled over the gate and raced to his sister's side.

She grabbed his hand and looked up at Patrick. "Now you can take us to the lifeboat!"

Patrick's stomach twisted. What would he do if Hamad wasn't allowed on a lifeboat? The crew members on the port deck were getting more short-tempered by the minute. Patrick understood. It was taking too long to move the passengers. Lifeboats were being lowered half-full. The emergency staircase that led to the C deck was already flooding. The lights that lit the steps glowed an eerie green under the seawater. They were running out of time.

But Hamad didn't wait for Patrick. He was already leading his sister through the crowd. Patrick and Ranger followed them to the deck.

When they arrived, a family was standing near lifeboat fourteen. The little girl was wrapped in a White Star Line blanket. Her mother wore a man's overcoat.

"Stay back!" an officer shouted to a man who was creeping forward.

"Let's go!" A steward took the girl from her parents and guided her to the lifeboat. "Now you, too!" he shouted to her mother. "Take a seat in the boat."

"Go, Lottie!" her husband shouted as the sailors pulled her toward the boat. "Go and be brave! I'll get a seat in another boat."

Patrick watched him step back into a crowd of other men. The man's grim face made it clear he knew the truth. There wouldn't be enough boats for everyone.

Patrick was about to ask one of the officers about Hamad when a teenaged boy jumped into the lifeboat beside the woman and her daughter. The women in the boat tried to help him, hiding him under their skirts.

One of the officers pointed a gun at the boy. "I'll give you ten seconds to get back onto that ship!"

The boy climbed back over the rail and collapsed onto the deck. Patrick turned away. He tried to tune out the sound of the boy's crying. But Maryam had seen what happened. She stared at the boy, and her eyes filled with tears.

Ranger licked Maryam's hand, but it didn't help. He didn't know what could make things better with everyone so upset. Hamad wasn't crying, but his eyes were big and scared. Ranger sat down beside him and leaned into him.

Maryam wiped her tears with her sleeve, just as a first-class lady arrived to board a lifeboat. She wore a long wool coat over her gown and a pile of hats on her head. Many people on deck wore layers of clothing, trying to save what they could from the flooding ship.

Maryam stared at that pile of hats. Then she broke away from Patrick and Hamad and raced to the woman's side.

"Maryam!" Patrick called. She was going to get herself in trouble again. "Come back!"

Maryam ignored him. She tugged on the woman's sleeve and said something. The woman looked surprised. Maryam pointed at Hamad, and the woman looked up. Her face softened. She nodded, took off one of her hats, and gave it to Maryam.

Maryam raced back to Hamad and held out the hat. "Hurry! Put this on your head!"

"What?" Hamad stared at the hat. It had a wide brim, with flowers and a bow piled on top.

"They won't let boys on the lifeboat," Maryam whispered. "So you will have to be a girl instead." With that, she shoved the hat onto his head.

Hamad began to protest. "I'm not wearing —" But Patrick cut him off.

"She's right," he said. "You can pass for a girl." He grabbed a blanket someone had left on the deck. He wrapped it around Hamad's shoulders and pulled the brim of the hat lower to hide his face. Patrick stepped back to look at Hamad.

Then he leaned close to the children and whispered, "Don't say another word now. This may be your only chance to get off the ship."

Chapter 11

HIDING IN PLAIN SIGHT

Lifeboat fourteen had already been lowered to the A deck. Patrick grabbed Hamad's and Maryam's hands and headed for the next boat. Crew members hurried past, shouting to one another.

"We need help on the boat deck!"

"Any more women down there?"

Patrick peered down to the deck below and caught a glimpse of Mr. Andrews. In the dim light, he and another man were tossing steamer chairs over the railing into the sea. Patrick frowned. What was the point? Getting rid of weight on the sinking ship wasn't going to keep it afloat. But then Patrick saw one of the chairs bobbing in the waves. A man who'd already fallen or jumped from the *Titanic* was swimming desperately toward it. Mr. Andrews wasn't throwing chairs overboard to get rid of weight on the ship; he was throwing them so people in the water could use them as rafts.

Patrick felt a chill that had nothing to do with the icy air. He looked around the ship, at the crowds of people and the few remaining lifeboats. There weren't even close to enough.

Patrick knew most crew members would be the last to leave. What would he do when the ship finally sank beneath the waves? Would he cling to the railing until the last possible second? Or would it be better to jump clear of the ship and hope to swim to a lifeboat or floating chair? Patrick shivered again. He couldn't imagine choosing that frigid black water.

"Will they let Hamad go in a boat now?" Maryam whispered up at Patrick.

"Yes," Patrick said, but he had no idea if the disguise would work. He pushed all of the cold-water thoughts from his mind and pulled the children toward the next boat. Ranger stayed close as they stepped up to the railing.

"I brought up two young sisters from third class," Patrick told the officer loading the boat.

"Have you, then?" the officer said. His eyes settled on Maryam, then drifted to Hamad. "Into the boat you go." The officer held a hand out to the children and helped them into the lifeboat. Two dozen passengers were already crowded into the little boat. A woman from Maryam and Hamad's village spotted them and reached up with her arms held out. Patrick prayed that she wouldn't call Hamad's name.

She didn't. She simply took Maryam's hand and helped her settle on the bench. Hamad sat by his sister and stared up at Patrick. Maryam lifted her hand in a quiet wave.

"Be safe!" Patrick called. "I'll . . ." He swallowed hard. "I'll see you when we get to New York." The last word stuck in his throat. He stepped back from the railing, wishing he could have said a better good-bye. There would be no grand arrival in New York, he understood now. Below in the waves, another lifeboat was pulling away. Soon, the last boats would follow, and there would be no hope for those who remained. Patrick would go down with the ship he'd helped to build.

"Lower aft!" an officer shouted as the crew maneuvered lifeboat fifteen down the side of the ship. "Lower stern! Now together!"

"Come on!" An officer clapped Patrick on the shoulder. "We've got a few to launch yet."

Patrick followed the officer and helped to load lifeboat two. With every minute that passed, the *Titanic* seemed to lurch a bit more. There were more shouts. More cries. More panic.

And there were still so many people on the ship. The air crackled with danger. Ranger smelled fear on every passenger's breath. How could he possibly help them all?

Chapter 12

DARKNESS AND ICE

Ranger stood close to the people who seemed most upset. A man who'd said good-bye to his wife and stood quietly weeping on the deck. A boy who was wailing because he hadn't been allowed to join his mother on the last boat. Ranger nuzzled the boy's hand and leaned against him. When you couldn't fix a problem, you could at least let a person know you were there.

Once lifeboat two was in the water, Patrick and the other crewmen moved on to the collapsible lifeboats. The band's music still drifted up from the deck below, but it was harder and harder to stay calm. Twice, Patrick lost his footing on the wet, sloping deck. Was that how this would end? Would he simply slide over the edge into the frigid sea?

Patrick crossed to the starboard side of the ship, where collapsible A was tied, and started hacking at its lines with a knife. As long as he did his job, he could distract himself. As long as he kept working and sweating, it was almost possible to imagine this was just another day at the shipyard and soon the whistle would send him home for supper.

Home. Patrick's breath caught in his throat. He'd told his mother he'd have a promotion in the shipyard when he returned. He couldn't die here in the North Atlantic!

Patrick blinked away the tears burning his eyes. "Hurry!" he called to a group of women huddled nearby. "Get in the boat!"

The whole ship lurched then. There was a sound like iron ripping apart.

"What's happening?" one of the women called out.

"She's coming apart!" a crewman shouted. The center of the ship was buckling. Water streamed down the decks.

"Hold on!"

Patrick grabbed a railing.

Ranger spread his toes as wide as he could. He'd done some of his search-and-rescue training on wet days. He'd practiced walking on slippery, uneven surfaces. But nothing like this.

People ran everywhere, slipping on the deck, clinging to the rails. Others huddled in tight little circles and prayed.

"Watch out!" someone shouted. Across the ship, crewmen tipped collapsible B off the roof of the officers' quarters onto the flooded boat deck. It landed upside down. Before it could be

righted, a rush of water surged over the deck and swept it into the sea.

Hundreds of people ran up the deck, trying to stay in the center so the rushing water wouldn't sweep them off the ship, too. Patrick spotted two men climbing way up to the stern of the boat. He stared as they climbed over the railing, held on, and then, one by one, let go. Did they have a chance of surviving in the freezing ocean?

"Quickly!" Patrick shouted as the last women boarded collapsible A.

The *Titanic* plunged again. A giant wave surged over the deck. The lifeboat was afloat, but still attached to its ropes like a dog on a too-tight leash.

"Cut the falls!" someone shouted. Crewmen hacked at the ropes with knives to free the boat while more passengers pushed forward, trying to climb in.

"Whoa!" A steward who'd gotten tangled in the ropes tripped and tumbled into the water.

The man cutting the rope on collapsible A hacked his way through the last fibers. Just then, another wave washed over the ship and swept him into the sea.

Ranger's paws slid on the deck. He tried to stay close to Patrick, but how could he possibly help? He couldn't stop the waves. He couldn't keep the ship afloat. He'd lost track of his first aid kit a long time ago, but it didn't matter. How could he go home when there was nothing he could do to save all these people?

Screams rose up from the water. Patrick clung to a railing. He tried to breathe, tried to think.

The rockets hadn't brought help. There was no rescue ship in sight. There were no more lifeboats. But there were wooden chairs in the water.

And boats that had launched half-full. They'd rescue people from the water. They'd have to.

Patrick took a deep, shaky breath. He'd have to jump. It was his best chance — his only chance — to see his mother again.

He found an abandoned life jacket on the deck and put it on. He took off his boots and emptied his pockets. Any extra weight would drag him down. But then he felt the little pouch with the pennies from his father, and his eyes burned with tears.

Ranger stepped up to Patrick and nuzzled his hand. It wasn't enough. Nothing would be enough on this awful, icy night.

But Patrick said, "Good dog . . . come on now . . ." He grabbed Ranger's collar and pulled him close. "We've got to jump," he whispered. "You and me. We'll go together."

Patrick took one of the pennies from the pouch and stared down at it in the moonlight.

If there was any luck in the little coin, he needed all of it. He tucked the penny deep into a pocket of his trousers. He left the other one in the pouch and tied that onto Ranger's collar. "They're lucky pennies, dog. This way, we both have one. And if I don't make it, then —" Patrick swallowed hard. "Then you'll have it to remember me."

Patrick clung to the railing with one hand as he climbed to the edge. With the other hand, he kept a firm grip on Ranger's collar. He tried to ignore the screams and cries coming from the water below. He peered down into the blackness. Then he let go of Ranger and climbed over, holding the railing tight. "Ready then, dog?"

He took a deep breath.

And let go.

Chapter 13

OVERBOARD!

Patrick disappeared over the edge of the ship, and Ranger knew what he had to do. He bounded over the railing, used his hind legs to push off into the dark sky, and plunged into the sea.

Ranger's belly smacked hard on the surface. Then the ocean swallowed him up. It was the coldest water Ranger had ever felt, like a thousand needles pricking under his fur. Ranger swam to the surface. He paddled as hard as he could. He tried to keep his face out of the water so he could breathe.

Above him, the ship was making horrible popping and cracking noises. The air smelled of dead fish and ice and terror. And people. So many people!

Ranger paddled through the sea of floating baggage and passengers. Some of the men swam toward lifeboats in the distance. One woman hoisted herself onto a decorated wooden wardrobe as it floated past. Others bobbed in their life jackets, screaming and crying into the dark. Ranger hated hearing so much hurt. But even worse were the ones who didn't make any sound at all.

The water felt colder and colder. With every minute that passed, more passengers went quiet. Where was Patrick?

Ranger barked. He was running out of time. He didn't know how long he could keep swimming. He couldn't feel his paws anymore. When a wooden chair floated past, Ranger scrambled up onto it. His hindquarters were still in the water, but it was better than nothing.

Ranger lifted his nose in the darkness, hoping to catch Patrick's scent. He could smell the icy ocean air and smoke coming from the sinking ship. Passengers floated all around him. Ranger could smell their perfume and their wet wool coats and their fear.

Finally . . . *there!*

The Patrick smell!

Ranger slipped off the floating chair and started swimming again. The smell went away, but then a wisp of wind brought it back. Ranger swam in that direction until he saw Patrick, bobbing in the water. He was quiet, and his eyes were closed.

Ranger paddled up to him and barked. He pawed at Patrick's life jacket and barked again.

Patrick opened his eyes. He reached for

Ranger. He couldn't speak. His teeth were chattering so hard they seemed like they might crumble to pieces. He needed to get out of the water.

Ranger barked and swam away from Patrick, toward the chair that was still floating nearby. But Patrick didn't follow him. Could he still swim?

Ranger paddled back to Patrick and poked at his face with a paw.

"Wh-wh-what?!" Patrick spit out a mouthful of seawater and blinked hard.

Ranger swam away. This time, he went all the way to the chair. He paddled up beside it and barked again.

A wooden chair! Patrick's heart leaped. He'd been certain he was going to die in this icy sea. Now, he took a trembling breath. The frozen air burned his lungs, but he had to find one last bit of strength.

Patrick reached out an arm and forced himself to start kicking. His whole body was numb, but somehow he was moving forward. When he reached the chair, he flung an arm over the seat and pulled the top half of his body out of the water.

That was all Patrick could do. Unless a rescue ship arrived soon, it wouldn't be enough to keep him alive. He was frozen and exhausted. He'd already given up back there, before the dog found him. He'd decided that he would close his eyes and just go to sleep. But now his arms and legs were awake and hurting again.

And the dog was here. Maybe he could hold on a little longer.

Ranger wanted to climb up next to Patrick and keep him warm, but he was afraid the whole chair would tip over. Patrick was so exhausted and cold, he might not have the strength to climb up again.

At least Ranger had fur. But he felt himself slowing down, too. He wouldn't be able to save Patrick by himself. He needed to find help.

That's what Ranger had learned to do in search-and-rescue training with Luke and Dad. He'd practiced finding Luke when Luke was pretending to be lost or hurt. Then Ranger would give an alert. He'd bark so Dad would come and find Luke, too. But tonight, there was no one left to help.

The big ship had tipped in the water. It was nearly vertical, with its stern pointing up at the night sky. The *Titanic* groaned and roared with explosions as its insides pulled apart. On the highest deck, ropes snapped. With a grinding roar, one of the towering funnels toppled over and slammed into the sea.

It sent a giant wave heading straight for them.

Ranger barked and pawed at Patrick's arm. He had to stay awake! He had to hold on!

Then the wave hit. It lifted their deck chair as if it were nothing more than a splinter.

When it splashed down again, Patrick was gone.

Chapter 14

LIGHTS ON THE HORIZON

Ranger swam all around the floating chair. Where was Patrick?

Ranger dived under the icy waves again and again. He could barely breathe, but he couldn't give up. He swam a wider circle, and finally . . . there!

Patrick was still afloat. He was trying to kick his way to an overturned lifeboat — one of the collapsibles that had washed into the sea. Five or six men were already balanced on top, trying to keep from toppling into the water.

But there was room for one more person. There had to be.

"C-c-co-come on. D-d-d-dog!" Patrick said. He tried to kick harder. He reached out his arm and pushed through the water. Again. And again. Until finally, it landed on the edge of the boat.

But a man shoved it off with his foot. "There's no room!" he said. The others seemed to be arguing behind him. The man turned to them. "Even one more could tip the boat and send us all to our deaths!" The other passengers quieted down, and two men started rowing away.

Patrick felt his hope slip away, too. The people on the boat wouldn't help. There was nothing left to do but go to sleep. But the dog wouldn't stop barking.

Ranger kept getting mouthfuls of seawater

as he struggled to keep himself afloat. Patrick had to get out of the water. If the people on the boat wouldn't help, Ranger would have to find someone else.

There were other little boats nearby. Ranger couldn't make Patrick swim to them. All he could do was bark. And he wasn't going to stop.

Finally, one of the lifeboats came closer. People were arguing in that boat, too. Ranger recognized two of their voices.

"But we have room!" a girl shouted. "We can't leave them!"

And then, a boy's voice. "Maryam, that's Patrick!"

Patrick's eyelids fluttered. Was he dreaming? Or was he staring up at the lifeboat that Maryam and Hamad had boarded?

"Absolutely not!" a man said. "There are hundreds of people in the water. What if they swamp the boat?"

"That's our friend!" Hamad shouted.

"We can't, children," a woman said quietly. "We just — "

Then there was a splash and a scream.

"She's jumped in!" the woman shouted. "Get that child in the boat!"

"Maryam!" Hamad called. "Come back!"

But Maryam was swimming away in her life jacket. Gasping for air, she reached out to Patrick and grabbed at his arm.

"Wh-wh-wha — " Patrick couldn't make his mouth work anymore.

"Swim!" Maryam coughed on a mouthful of ocean. "Come on!" she sobbed. But Patrick closed his eyes.

Ranger paddled over to Patrick and licked his cheek. It tasted salty, a mix of seawater and frozen tears.

Patrick couldn't feel the dog's tongue on his cheek, but he breathed in Ranger's warm breath.

He opened his eyes. Ranger was there. And Maryam.

He wouldn't give up. Not yet.

Patrick reached out and started to swim. He couldn't even tell if his frozen legs were kicking, but little by little, he moved forward. Maryam and Ranger swam behind him.

When they got to the boat, a man reached out to grab Maryam, but she pushed herself back. "You have to help my friend!" she cried.

"For goodness' sake, get them both in the boat!" a woman cried. The men argued, but two other women overruled them. They reached down, grabbed Patrick's arms, and dragged him onto the floor of the boat. Maryam landed next to him, and one of the women wrapped them both in a thick wool blanket.

Ranger was still in the water.

"D-d-d-dog . . ." Patrick tried to point, but the men were already rowing away.

Then there was a ripping sound louder than any of the others. The men stopped rowing. Everyone stared as *Titanic* split in half. A shower of sparks exploded into the sea. Two more funnels came crashing down, and the great ship's stern rose higher into the night sky. It hung there for a moment. Then it sank, faster and faster, until even the flag on the stern was swallowed up by the sea.

Patrick couldn't believe what he'd seen. It wasn't a dream.

The great ship was gone. Every beam his father had laid. Every rivet he'd helped to place in her sides. Every gleaming chandelier.

Gone.

The men in the lifeboat started rowing again.

"Where did the dog go?" Maryam said.

Patrick squinted into the darkness. He couldn't see Ranger anymore. He whispered a quiet "thank you" into the night. And hoped, somehow, the dog would be all right.

Ranger was already paddling away from the lifeboat. He found his way back to the floating deck chair and scrambled up onto the seat. There was more room now, with Patrick on the lifeboat. But there was nothing else he could do to help. He heard cries in the distance, but they faded away as the night dragged on. The lifeboats had rowed away. The people in the water around him were all quiet.

Finally, Ranger saw lights approaching in the darkness. They were hazy at first but grew stronger and nearer. It was a ship. A big one, coming to rescue Patrick and Maryam and

Hamad and all the people in the little boats. Distant cheers and cries of relief floated over the water from far away.

And then Ranger heard another sound. A quiet humming.

It took him a little while to spot it, but there, amid the floating furniture and hat-boxes, was his first aid kit. Ranger slipped into the water and paddled toward it. The humming was already getting louder. Beams of light spilled from the cracks in the box and danced on the black water.

Ranger ducked his head under and brought it up with the old leather strap around his neck. The box grew warm at Ranger's throat, and heat spread over him like a warm bath.

The humming grew louder and louder. Ranger felt as if he were being squeezed through a hole in the sky. The light from the cracks was so bright he couldn't see the ship in the distance anymore. It grew so bright that he had to close his eyes.

When he opened them, Luke and Sadie were walking into the mudroom with their life jackets.

Chapter 15

BACK ON LAND

Ranger lowered his head and let his first aid kit drop onto his dog bed just as Luke knelt beside him.

"Hey, Ranger!" Luke said, giving him a scratch behind his ear. "Did you miss us?"

Ranger nuzzled Luke's hand. He had never been so happy to be warm, and dry, and home.

"You missed a good picnic," Sadie said. "I saved you a little of my lunch." She rummaged through her bag and pulled out a triangle of a ham sandwich. Ranger wolfed it down in one bite.

"Hey, what's this?" Luke leaned over and tugged at the little pouch on Ranger's collar. He untied it, loosened the drawstring, and pulled it open. "A penny?" He tipped the pouch so the little coin fell into his palm.

"That's a weird penny," Sadie said.

Luke squinted at it. "It's old. And it's from somewhere else. Maybe Zeeshan and Noreen gave it to him. They visited Europe last summer, didn't they?"

Ranger pawed at Luke's hand. Luke laughed and tucked the coin into its pouch. "Don't worry. I'm giving it back," he said. He dropped it into Ranger's dog bed and turned to Sadie. "Let's get the boat stuff cleaned up so we can go outside before dinner." They headed to the shed to put their life jackets away.

Carefully, Ranger picked up the little pouch in his teeth. He pawed at the blanket on his dog bed until he uncovered his other treasures — all gifts from the children he'd helped on his journeys. There was a little quilt square, a funny-shaped leaf, and a piece of an old metal brooch. There were two feathers — one brown and white, and one bright yellow — and a folded-up scrap of paper that smelled of seawater and sand.

Ranger dropped the little pouch with the penny beside them. He pawed at his blanket until everything was covered up. Then he flopped down in his bed to rest. It felt good to be warm. He was so glad his job was finally done. Somehow, he knew that Patrick and Maryam and Hamad were safe and dry now, too.

Luke and Sadie came running back inside. "That was so much fun today!" Sadie said.

"Sure was," Luke said. He knelt beside Ranger, and stroked the fur on his neck. "You missed a great day, Ranger. We went tubing

and dropped anchor near an island in the lake and jumped off the rocks." Luke sighed. "I wish you liked boats more. Then you could have had an adventure, too."

Ranger yawned and snuggled into his blanket. Tomorrow, he'd go outside with Luke and Sadie and chase some squirrels. And that would be adventure enough.

AUTHOR'S NOTE

The sinking of the *Titanic* is one of the most famous disasters in history. I'd read about it when I was in school and thought I knew the story, but when I began my research for this book, I discovered that the details I'd heard were only the beginning.

Most people know about the passengers who lost their lives when the *Titanic* sank in the North Atlantic, but few stop to think about the shipbuilders who died before it even set sail. Shipyards of the early 1900s were risky places to work. Harland and Wolff in Belfast, Ireland, was no exception.

Men worked from six in the morning to five thirty in the evening with two short breaks for breakfast and lunch. Conditions were loud, crowded, and dangerous. Falls were common. Men could be hit by cranes or crushed by falling plates. Wind could make the scaffolding collapse.

Harland and Wolff shipyard recorded 254 accidents while the *Titanic* was being built. Eight of those were fatal, like the accident that claimed the life of Patrick's father in this story.

Today, the site of that shipyard is a world-class museum, dedicated to telling the story of the building and the sinking of the *Titanic*.

Men worked from six in the morning to five thirty in the evening with two short breaks for breakfast and lunch. Conditions were loud, crowded, and dangerous. Falls were common. Men could be hit by cranes or crushed by falling plates. Wind could make the scaffolding collapse.

Harland and Wolff shipyard recorded 254 accidents while the *Titanic* was being built. Eight of those were fatal, like the accident that claimed the life of Patrick's father in this story.

Today, the site of that shipyard is a world-class museum, dedicated to telling the story of the building and the sinking of the *Titanic*.

AUTHOR'S NOTE

The sinking of the *Titanic* is one of the most famous disasters in history. I'd read about it when I was in school and thought I knew the story, but when I began my research for this book, I discovered that the details I'd heard were only the beginning.

Most people know about the passengers who lost their lives when the *Titanic* sank in the North Atlantic, but few stop to think about the shipbuilders who died before it even set sail. Shipyards of the early 1900s were risky places to work. Harland and Wolff in Belfast, Ireland, was no exception.

Construction of the *Titanic* began in late March of 1909. When it was finished two years later, it weighed 46,328 tons. The great ship was 882 feet long and 92 feet wide. The *Titanic*'s launch happened on May 31, 1911, with a hundred thousand people watching. But there were many jobs still to be done — painting, woodworking, bringing in furniture and supplies.

On April 2, 1912, the ship set sail on its maiden voyage. Like Patrick, a number of men who'd helped to build the ship were invited on that trip, in case there was last-minute work to be done along the way. After the *Titanic* left Belfast, it went through sea trials, a series of tests to make sure everything was working properly. Then, before crossing the Atlantic, it made three stops to pick up passengers — in Southampton, England; Cherbourg, France;

and Queensland, Ireland. Those passengers came from many different countries. Some, like Patrick, were from Ireland. Others came from England, Germany, Sweden, and Norway. Hamad's and Maryam's characters in this book are based loosely on the stories of more than eighty *Titanic* passengers who came from villages in Lebanon. They were laborers, housekeepers, farmers, and families, hoping for a better life in America.

In addition to the *Titanic*'s human passengers, there were also animals on board when the ship set sail. The story of Jenny the cat is based on first-person accounts from people who remember seeing her on the ship and then leaving with her kittens when it docked in Southampton. Records show there were likely twelve dogs on board, too. Among them was at least one French bulldog being brought home by an American who'd been visiting Paris. Other canine passengers reportedly included a Pomeranian, a chow chow, a King Charles spaniel, and a lapdog named Frou-Frou. There was also an Airedale named Kitty, owned by the millionaire John Jacob Astor, and a Pekingese named Sun Yat-sen, after the president of China. Three of the smaller dogs survived by escaping in lifeboats with their owners.

The main characters in *Ranger in Time: Disaster on the* Titanic — Patrick, Hamad, and Maryam — are fictional, but they're based on real passengers and crew members who were on board the ship. Some of the minor characters in this story were real people. Mr. Andrews, the ship designer Patrick watches through the big drawing room windows in chapter 1, is Thomas Andrews, who designed the *Titanic*. Andrews was on board the ship and died when it sank. According to survivors' accounts, he really did toss steamer chairs overboard and run around the decks, urging people to get in the lifeboats.

The scene in chapter 10, where a man tells his wife, "Go, Lottie! Go and be brave! I'll get a seat in another boat," also features real passengers from the *Titanic*. "Lottie" was Charlotte Collyer, a second-class passenger who was traveling with her husband, Harvey, and her eight-year-old daughter, Marjorie. Charlotte and Marjorie survived, but Mr. Collyer never found that seat in another boat. He was one of more than 1,500 people who died when the *Titanic* sank. The timeline of events that led to the ship sinking in this story is also based on historical documents.

According to survivors' accounts, there really were arguments in the lifeboats that night. Some people fought to go back to the ship to rescue those in the water. Others feared that so many desperate, frightened people would overwhelm the lifeboats and they'd capsize. So even though there was room in many of the lifeboats, few people were rescued after the ship went down.

Whether or not a passenger survived depended largely on who they were and how they were traveling. Men were ordered to let women and children board the lifeboats first, so only around 20 percent of the men on the *Titanic* survived, compared to about 74 percent of the women. First-class passengers were also more likely to survive. When the iceberg hit, crew members woke them up and brought them to the boat deck first. Third-class passengers had to wait. Many didn't speak English, so they didn't understand the warnings and directions. About 62 percent of the *Titanic*'s first-class passengers were rescued that night. Approximately 41 percent of its second-class passengers survived, compared to just around 25 percent of those traveling in third class.

Even those who were lucky enough to make it into lifeboats had to wait hours for the *Carpathia*, the ship that rescued the *Titanic*'s survivors, to arrive. Survivors climbed up rope ladders that were lowered into the lifeboats. Some of the children were reportedly brought up in cloth sacks. This display from the *Titanic* museum in Belfast shows some of the *Titanic*'s survivors in lifeboats and on board the *Carpathia* after they were rescued.

The lucky penny that Patrick gives Ranger was inspired by the real story of Thomas Millar, an assistant deck engineer on the *Titanic*. Millar had joined the crew of the big ship after his wife died, leaving him with two young sons to raise. Millar had hoped he could build a new life in New York, so he left his sons with an aunt and promised to send for them once he was settled in America. According to a story shared later by Millar's grandson, and published in Titanic: *Belfast's Own* by Stephen Cameron, Millar gave each boy two shiny, new 1912 pennies before he left on the trip. "They're this year's," he said. "Don't spend them until I get back."

Millar was one of those who died when *Titanic* sank. His older son never spent his two pennies.

FURTHER READING

If you'd like to read more about the *Titanic* and about working dogs like Ranger, here are some books and websites you might find interesting:

DK Eyewitness Books: Titanic by Simon Adams (DK Eyewitness Books, 2014)

882 1/2 Amazing Answers to Your Questions about the Titanic by Hugh Brewster and Laurie Coulter (Scholastic Paperbacks, 1999)

I Survived the Sinking of the Titanic, *1912* by Lauren Tarshis (Scholastic, 2010)

Lost Liners: *Titanic* from PBS: www.pbs.org /lostliners/titanic.html

Remembering the *Titanic* from National Geographic Kids: http://kids.national geographic.com/explore/history/a-titanic -anniversary/#TitanicInterior1.jpg

Sniffer Dogs: How Dogs (and Their Noses) Save the World by Nancy Castaldo (Houghton Mifflin Harcourt, 2014)

Titanic: *Voices from the Disaster* by Deborah Hopkinson (Scholastic, 2012)

SOURCES

I'm most grateful to the staff and historians of Titanic Belfast, who answered my questions and pointed me to various resources in the museum. The following sources were also helpful:

Blair, William. Titanic: *Behind the Legend*. Belfast: National Museums Northern Ireland, 2012.

Cameron, Stephen. Titanic: *Belfast's Own*. Newtownards, Northern Ireland: Colourpoint Books, 2011.

Elias, Leila Salloum. "Alien Passengers: Syrians Aboard the *Titanic*." *Jerusalem Quarterly* Issue 52 (2013): 51-67, http://www.palestine-studies.org/sites/default/files/jq-articles/JQ-52-Salloum-Alien_Passengers_2.pdf

Hutchings, David F., and Richard de Kerbrech. *RMS* Titanic *Owners' Workshop Manual: An Insight into the Design, Engineering, Construction and History of the Most Famous Passenger Ship of All Time*. Sparkford, Yeovil Somerset, UK: Haynes Publishing, 2014.

Lord, Walter. *A Night to Remember: The Classic Account of the Final Hours of the* Titanic. New York: St. Martin's Griffin, 1955.

Mayo, Jonathan. Titanic: *Minute by Minute*. London: Short Books, 2016.

O'Donnell, E. E. *Father Browne's* Titanic *Album: A Passenger's Photographs and Personal Memoir*. Dublin: Messenger Publications, 2011.

White, John D. T. *The RMS* Titanic *Miscellany*. Dublin: Irish Academic Press, 2011.

Wilson, Andrew. *Shadow of the* Titanic: *The Extraordinary Stories of Those Who Survived*. New York: Simon & Schuster, 2011.

ABOUT THE AUTHOR

Kate Messner is the author of *Breakout*; *The Seventh Wish*; *All the Answers*; *The Brilliant Fall of Gianna Z.*, recipient of the E. B. White Read Aloud Award for Older Readers; *Capture the Flag*, a Crystal Kite Award winner; *Over and Under the Snow*, a *New York Times* Notable Children's Book; and the Ranger in Time and Marty McGuire chapter book series. A former middle-school English teacher, Kate lives on Lake Champlain with her family and loves reading, walking in the woods, and traveling. Visit her online at katemessner.com.

DON'T MISS RANGER'S NEXT ADVENTURE!

It's 1776 and the Revolutionary War is raging! Ranger's new friend Isaac Pope is a young soldier in the Continental army. And when General George Washington needs a spy to cross into enemy territory, Isaac is chosen for the dangerous task. Now Ranger must keep Isaac safe and the Patriots' plans undetected or the battle will surely be lost. Turn the page for a sneak peek!

Isaac Pope held the flat-bottomed boat steady while soldiers waded into the river and loaded supplies.

"Quickly!" an officer whispered through the pounding rain. "We must have every man across before dawn!"

Isaac nodded. The men were forbidden to speak. This mission had to be silent and secret. Anything else would mean disaster.

The boat sank lower in the water until Isaac signaled that it was full. He and the other sailors used poles to push off from shore.

Their task felt impossible: Ferry nine thousand troops across the mile-long stretch of river between Long Island and New York. Horses and supplies had to be moved, too. All before the sun came up and British troops realized the rebel soldiers were fleeing. Anyone left behind would be taken prisoner.

Isaac felt dizzy. He imagined the Redcoats waking at first light to find hundreds of Continental soldiers trapped in Brooklyn. Isaac's ears still rang from the gunfire of the day before. He had crouched behind a stone wall, his heart pounding against the musket he held tight to his chest.

They'd fought bravely, but how long could they go on? George Washington's troops were beaten down. They'd held out for two days against an army twice their size. But now they were surrounded.

Could they possibly escape before dawn?

MEET RANGER

A time–traveling golden retriever with search-and-rescue training . . . and a nose for danger!

📖 **SCHOLASTIC**

scholastic.com

RANGER10